Famous Bears & Friends

ONE HUNDRED YEARS

~ of ~

Teddy Bear Stories,
Poems, Songs,
and
Heroics

written
and
collected
by

JANET WYMAN COLEMAN

DUTTON CHILDREN'S BOOKS
New York

To family who behave like friends and friends who feel like family,
especially my parents, Billy, Brooke, Will, and Susan Van Metre

WITH THANKS FOR THEIR EXPERTISE, PATIENCE, AND SUPPORT:

Susan Cohen, Susan Goodman, Lisa Jahn-Clough, Liza Ketchum, and Wallace F. Dailey at the Theodore Roosevelt Collection, Harvard College Library; Dr. Peter Thwaites and Jim Farrar at the Royal Military Academy Sandhurst; Michael Bond; Leyla Maniera at Steiff GmbH; Bruce Burdett at the *Sakonnet Times;* Rick Spencer at NASA Headquarters Library; Dr. Chiaki Mukai and the National Space Development Agency of Japan; T. Inoue and J. Kanegawa at Matsushita Electric Industrial Company, Ltd.; Daniel Agnew at Christie's South Kensington; Andrew D. Hartley; Catherine Howell at the Bethnal Green Museum of Childhood in London, England; and Virginia Durfee. I also wish to thank Theodore Roosevelt IV; Carl W. Haffenreffer for his photos of the Teddy Bear Invasion; Dianne Stott at Woodstock Woolly Bears; Dina and Nalene Denning at Creative Stitches; Dianne Liddic at the Crafty Frog; Les Smith and the artists at the Teddy Bear Rally; Cal Workman at the Vermont Teddy Bear Company; Jennifer Upton, Philip Hind, and everyone at the Weston and Wayland public libraries.

Library of Congress Cataloging-in-Publication Data

Famous bears and friends : one hundred years of teddy bear stories, poems, songs, and heroics / written and collected by Janet Wyman Coleman.

p. cm.

Summary: A collection of stories, poems, and historical information featuring famous teddy bears.

ISBN 0-525-46925-7 (Hardcover)

1. Teddy bears—Literary collections. [1. Teddy bears—Literary collections.] I. Coleman, Janet Wyman.

PZ5 .F21456 2002   808.8'0355   [Fic]—dc21   2002002592

Published in the United States 2002 by Dutton Children's Books, a division of Penguin Putnam Books for Young Readers

345 Hudson Street, New York, New York 10014

www.penguinputnam.com

Designed by Heather Wood • Printed in China

First Edition

2   4   6   8   10   9   7   5   3   1

All possible care has been taken to trace the ownership of all quotations and photographic images included herein
and to make full acknowledgment for their use. If any errors have accidentally occurred,
they will be corrected in subsequent editions, provided notification is sent to the publisher.

p. 5: Photos courtesy of the Theodore Roosevelt Collection, Harvard College Library. From the April 1924 issue of *Outdoor America,* published by the Izaak Walton League of America; p. 6: political cartoon by Clifford K. Berryman © 1902, *The Washington Post.* Reprinted with permission; p. 7: photo courtesy of the National Museum of American History, Smithsonian Institution; pp. 8–9: photos courtesy of Steiff GmbH; pp. 10–17: from *Winnie-the-Pooh,* copyright © 1926 by E. P. Dutton & Co., Inc.; copyright renewal 1954 by A. A. Milne; p. 19: photo of Lieutenant Harry D. Colebourn and bear cub, Collection 9 (N10467). Reprinted with permission of The Provincial Archives of Manitoba; photo of the original A. A. Milne stuffed animals, courtesy of the collection of the Central Children's Room, Donnell Library Center, The New York Public Library; pp. 20–23: from *When We Were Very Young,* copyright © 1924 by E. P. Dutton & Co., Inc.; copyright renewal 1952 by A. A. Milne; pp. 24–25: from *Now We Are Six,* copyright © 1927 by E. P. Dutton & Co., Inc.; copyright renewal 1955 by A. A. Milne; p. 26: photo courtesy of the Museum of Childhood, Ribchester, England; p. 27: photo used by permission of Jim Farrar, military photographer, Royal Military Academy Sandhurst; pp. 28–31: illustrations copyright © 2002 by Bernadette Pons; pp. 32–40: from *A Bear Called Paddington,* by Michael Bond, illustrated by Peggy Fortnum. Copyright © 1958, renewed 1986 by Michael Bond. Reprinted by permission of Houghton Mifflin Company. All rights reserved; p. 41: photo courtesy of Michael Bond; pp. 42–43: illustrations copyright © 2002 by Elisabeth Schlossberg; p. 44: "Hat," from *Where the Sidewalk Ends,* by Shel Silverstein. Copyright © 1974 by Evil Eye Music, Inc. Used by permission of HarperCollins Publishers; p. 45: "Teddy Bear Poem," reprinted with permission of Atheneum Books for Young Readers, from *If I Were in Charge of the World and Other Worries,* by Judith Viorst. Text copyright © 1981 Judith Viorst; pp. 44–45: illustrations copyright © 2002 by Thea Kliros; p. 46: photo reprinted with permission of *The Daily Hampshire Gazette.* All rights reserved; p. 47: photo of black "mourning" bear, used by permission of Christie's South Kensington, Teddy Bear Department; photo of Karen Braithwaite and her bear, by Ruth Fremson/NYT Pictures, used by permission of *The New York Times* Photo Archives, *The New York Times* Agency; pp. 48–57: *Corduroy,* reprinted with permission of Viking Children's Books. Text copyright © 1968 by Don Freeman; p. 58: photo courtesy of Viking Children's Books; p. 59: photos courtesy of Dianne Stott; p. 60: photos of Pete and Repeat and Trapeze Girl courtesy of Janet Wyman Coleman; photo of teddy bear enthusiast reprinted with permission of *The Daily Hampshire Gazette.* All rights reserved; p. 61: photo courtesy of National Space Development Agency of Japan; p. 62: photo courtesy of Matsushita Electric Industrial Company, Ltd.

· C O N T E N T S ·

Teddy's Bear

An Introduction

You are holding a book filled with teddy bears. A few of the bears are quite famous: Winnie-the-Pooh, Paddington from Darkest Peru, and Corduroy, who just needs a button. The others have names you may not recognize, but their adventures are incredible. One teddy bear floated in space; another plunged into the icy North Atlantic. Senior Under Officer Edward Bear parachuted out of a plane, and a robotic bear named Kuma sings in Japanese. They're all here, waiting for you.

The bears have gathered to celebrate their one hundredth birthday. From their beginnings in a small shop in Brooklyn, New York, and a German toy factory, they have traveled to homes around the world. Every night millions of teddy bears are tucked under the covers in millions of beds. They make the darkness less frightening, and we become braver in their company. Teddy bears hear our secrets and never whisper a word. More than any other toy, they offer understanding, comfort, and friendship. Of course, teddy bears love the happy times, too. Think of all the birthday parties they have attended. Isn't it time they had one of their own?

Do you have a teddy bear? Does he like adventures? If so, pull him close and read these stories together.

The President and the Stuffed Bear

At 4:00 P.M. on November 13, 1902, President Theodore Roosevelt stepped off a train in Smedes, Mississippi. He wore a fringed hunting suit and carried a Winchester rifle. His favorite ivory-handled hunting knife hung from a belt. A crowd of people surrounded the train, some standing and others sitting on cotton bales. They had waited for hours in a cold drizzle to see the president of the United States.

Roosevelt had traveled to Mississippi to settle a dispute between the state and its neighbor Louisiana over the position of their shared border. He also wanted to learn more about the tensions between black and white Americans. Many blacks in Mississippi were former slaves, and they strug-

President Roosevelt (holding a rifle) and fellow hunters on the Mississippi bear hunt of 1902

That night, Roosevelt and the others sat at a campfire on the edge of the river. They ate candied sweet potatoes and turkey hashes. As the firelight played across their faces, the president asked Holt Collier about his life as a slave. A reporter on the trip described Collier's response: "[He spoke] simply and fearlessly, as became one who knew…he was no less of a man than any of the officials or planters or lawyers or brokers about him."

The next day, Holt Collier climbed on a horse and followed sixty hunting dogs into the Mississippi swamp. Reluctantly, the president agreed to wait nearby while the dogs searched the dense underbrush for the scent of a bear.

gled to be treated fairly by the white population. The president, who was a famous hunter, also planned to go on a six-day bear hunt.

The hunting party rode fifteen miles by horseback to a camp at the edge of the Little Sunflower River. There Roosevelt met Holt Collier, a former slave who was known as the best bear tracker in the Mississippi Delta. Collier had led hunters to more than sixteen hundred bears, one hundred and fifty in a single season. The politicians who had organized the hunt wanted to ensure that the president shot a bear.

Holt Collier, a former slave, who was the best bear tracker in the Mississippi Delta

DRAWING
THE LINE
IN MISSISSIPPI

The political cartoon by Clifford K. Berryman that led to the birth of the teddy bear in America

Soon they picked up a trail, but still the president had to wait late into the afternoon as the pack followed their prey. In and out of the river they swarmed after the bear, forcing it to swim back and forth several times. The 235-pound animal killed one of Collier's favorite dogs before the tracker succeeded in roping it to a tree. He blew his horn to alert the hunting party and sent a young helper to get the president.

When Roosevelt arrived, he discovered "a bear with his tongue lolling out...sitting halfway up in the mud, swaying from side to side helplessly." To the amazement of the hunting party, the president refused to shoot the animal, because he felt that it wasn't sporting to gun down an exhausted bear tied to a tree.

The correspondents accompanying the president sent their reports back to New York and Washington, D.C. Two days later *The Washington Post* carried a political cartoon by Clifford K. Berryman that showed the president refusing to shoot a small bear. The cartoon was captioned, "Drawing the Line in Mississippi." The title referred not only to Roosevelt's decision not to shoot the bear but also to the dispute about the Mississippi-Louisiana state line.

Two Russian immigrants living in Brooklyn, New York, saw Berryman's cartoon and had a wonderful idea. Rose and Morris Michtom ran a small store that sold candy and handmade toys, and soon Rose was sewing two bears with black shoe-button eyes and straw stuffing. The Michtoms displayed the bears in the window of their store with the cartoon and a small sign that said TEDDY'S BEAR. (Teddy was Theodore Roosevelt's nickname.)

An early Ideal teddy bear given by the Michtoms' son to President Roosevelt's grandson on the teddy bear's sixtieth birthday

By the end of the first day, the Michtoms had sold the bears and had orders for twelve more. According to teddy bear legend, Morris Michtom made a bear and sent it to the president along with a letter asking permission to use his name. Roosevelt is said to have replied, "Dear Mr. Michtom, I don't think my name is likely to be worth much in the toy bear business, but you are welcome to use it." (Neither letter has ever been found. Perhaps it is just a good story.)

The "teddy bears," as they came to be known, were so popular that the Michtoms closed their store and began sewing the soft toys full-time. In 1903, they named their new business the Ideal Novelty and Toy Company. Within a few years, the company would produce thousands of teddy bears, and Teddy Roosevelt, a fierce and courageous hunter of grizzly bears, elephants, and rhinos, would become linked to a cuddly toy.

The Seamstress and the Teddy Bear Empire

Inside the Steiff toy factory at Giengen, the birthplace of millions and millions of teddy bears

When Margarete Steiff was a little girl, she rode to and from school in a small wooden cart, pulled by her sisters and friends. Her legs had been paralyzed by a disease called polio, and she was unable to walk.

A disabled young woman living in Germany in the 1860s faced a grim future, but Margarete Steiff was a remarkable person. She taught herself to play a stringed instrument, the zither, and gave lessons from her home. Soon she raised enough money to buy a sewing machine. The polio had weakened her right arm, so she ran the machine backward. Instead of pushing the material under the needle with her right hand, she pulled it with her left.

Margarete Steiff, the disabled woman who created a world-famous stuffed bear

Margarete Steiff sewed clothing for women and children and sold the items from a small shop. One day she made herself an elephant-shaped pincushion, which quickly became a favorite plaything of her nieces and nephews. So she sewed more elephants, and then monkeys, pigs, and camels. At the time, toys were made of wood, metal, and other hard materials, so these huggable, soft toys had unique appeal. Demand was so great that Steiff decided to open a toy factory. Businesswomen were rare in the nineteenth century, but a disabled woman running her own factory was extraordinary.

Several of Margarete Steiff's relatives became involved in the business. Her nephew Richard, inspired by animals he had seen at the zoo in Stuttgart, Germany, encouraged his aunt to make a stuffed bear. Richard drew sketches for a toy sewn out of mohair, a fabric made from the silky hair of

As teddy bears evolved, they looked more and more like babies and less like animals from the forest

Richard Steiff stares at the toy that will make the Steiff name immortal

An early Steiff bear (circa 1904) who looks as if he has a question

Angora goats, but Margarete Steiff didn't like the idea—mohair was far too expensive and difficult to obtain. Fortunately, Richard prevailed.

In 1903, Richard Steiff took his bear to the Leipzig Toy Fair. There he showed it to potential buyers from Europe and America. Most people thought the "bear doll," with its movable arms and legs, was very strange. Bears were fierce animals, after all. Why would a mother want one lying next to her child? One man disagreed and ordered three thousand stuffed bears for stores in America.

Some people insist that Margarete Steiff invented the teddy bear. Others claim that it was the Michtoms. Everyone agrees that a stuffed bear was born on both sides of the Atlantic at about the same time, and it became the teddy bear.

By 1908, the Steiff Company was producing almost a million bears a year. Steiff bears are still made today and are highly prized by children and adult collectors. Although Margarete Steiff couldn't walk, her famous teddy bears have traveled around the world.

·WINNIE-THE-POOH·

Winnie-the-Pooh and Some Bees

by A. A. Milne
with decorations by Ernest H. Shepard

Here is Edward Bear, coming downstairs now, bump, bump, bump, on the back of his head, behind Christopher Robin. It is, as far as he knows, the only way of coming downstairs, but sometimes he feels that there really is another way, if only he could stop bumping for a moment and think of it. And then he feels that perhaps there isn't. Anyhow, here he is at the bottom, and ready to be introduced to you. Winnie-the Pooh.

When I first heard his name, I said, just as you are going to say, "But I thought he was a boy?"

"So did I," said Christopher Robin.

"Then you can't call him Winnie?"

"I don't."

"But you said——"

"He's Winnie-ther-Pooh. Don't you know what *'ther'* means?"

"Ah, yes, now I do," I said quickly; and I hope you do too, because it is all the explanation you are going to get.

Sometimes Winnie-the-Pooh likes a game of some sort when he comes downstairs, and sometimes he likes to sit quietly in front of the fire and listen to a story. This evening——

"What about a story?" said Christopher Robin.

"*What* about a story?" I said.

"Could you very sweetly tell Winnie-the-Pooh one?"

"I suppose I could," I said. "What sort of stories does he like?"

"About himself. Because he's *that* sort of Bear."

"Oh, I see."

"So could you very sweetly?"

"I'll try," I said.

So I tried.

Once upon a time, a very long time ago now, about last Friday, Winnie-the-Pooh lived in a forest all by himself under the name of Sanders.

(*"What does 'under the name' mean?" asked Christopher Robin.*

"It means he had the name over the door in gold letters, and lived under it."

"Winnie-the-Pooh wasn't quite sure," said Christopher Robin.

"Now I am," said a growly voice.

"Then I will go on," said I.)

One day when he was out walking, he came to an open place in the middle of the forest, and in the middle of this place was a large oak-tree, and, from the top of the tree, there came a loud buzzing-noise.

Winnie-the-Pooh sat down at the foot of the tree, put his head between his paws and began to think.

First of all he said to himself: "That buzzing-noise means something. You don't get a buzzing-noise like that, just buzzing and buzzing, without its meaning something. If there's a buzzing-noise, somebody's making a buzzing-noise, and the only reason for making a buzzing-noise that *I* know of is because you're a bee."

Then he thought another long time, and said: "And the only reason for being a bee that I know of is making honey."

And then he got up, and said: "And the only reason for making honey is so as *I* can eat it." So he began to climb the tree.

He climbed and he climbed and he climbed, and as he climbed he sang a little song to himself. It went like this:

Isn't it funny
How a bear likes honey?
Buzz! Buzz! Buzz!
I wonder why he does?

Then he climbed a little further . . . and a little further . . . and then just a little further. By that time he had thought of another song.

It's a very funny thought that, if Bears were Bees,
They'd build their nests at the *bottom* of trees.
And that being so (if the Bees were Bears),
We shouldn't have to climb up all these stairs.

He was getting rather tired by this time, so that is why he sang a Complaining Song. He was nearly there now, and if he stood on that branch . . .

Crack!

"Oh, help!" said Pooh, as he dropped ten feet on the branch below him.

"If only I hadn't——" he said, as he bounced twenty feet on to the next branch.

"You see, what I *meant* to do," he explained, as he turned head-over-heels, and crashed on to another branch thirty feet below, "what I *meant* to do——"

"Of course, it *was* rather——" he admitted, as he slithered very quickly through the next six branches.

"It all comes, I suppose," he decided, as he said good-bye to the last branch, spun round three times, and flew gracefully into a gorse-bush, "it all comes of *liking* honey so much. Oh, help!"

He crawled out of the gorse-bush, brushed the prickles from his nose, and began to think again. And the first person he thought of was Christopher Robin.

(*"Was that me?" said Christopher Robin in an awed voice, hardly daring to believe it.*

"That was you."

Christopher Robin said nothing, but his eyes got larger and larger, and his face got pinker and pinker.)

So Winnie-the-Pooh went round to his friend Christopher Robin, who lived behind a green door in another part of the forest.

"Good morning, Christopher Robin," he said.

"Good morning, Winnie-*ther*-Pooh," said you.

"I wonder if you've got such a thing as a balloon about you?"

"A balloon?"

"Yes, I just said to myself coming along: 'I wonder if Christopher Robin has such a thing as a balloon about him?' I just said it to myself, thinking of balloons, and wondering."

"What do you want a balloon for?" you said.

Winnie-the-Pooh looked round to see that nobody was listening, put his paw to his mouth, and said in a deep whisper: *"Honey!"*

"But you don't get honey with balloons!"

"*I* do," said Pooh.

Well, it just happened that you had been to a party the day before at the house of your friend Piglet, and you had balloons at the party. You had had a big green balloon; and one of Rabbit's relations had had a big blue one, and had left it behind, being really too young to go to a party at all; and so you had brought the green one *and* the blue one home with you.

"Which one would you like?" you asked Pooh.

He put his head between his paws and thought very carefully.

"It's like this," he said. "When you go after

honey with a balloon, the great thing is not to let the bees know you're coming. Now, if you have a green balloon, they might think you were only part of the tree, and not notice you, and if you have a blue balloon, they might think you were only part of the sky, and not notice you, and the question is: Which is most likely?"

"Wouldn't they notice *you* underneath the balloon?" you asked.

"They might or they might not," said Winnie-the-Pooh. "You never can tell with bees." He thought for a moment and said: "I shall try to look like a small black cloud. That will deceive them."

"Then you had better have the blue balloon," you said; and so it was decided.

Well, you both went out with the blue balloon, and you took your gun with you, just in case, as you always did, and Winnie-the-Pooh went to a very muddy place that he knew of, and rolled and rolled until he was black all over; and then, when the balloon was blown up as big as

big, and you and Pooh were both holding on to the string, you let go suddenly, and Pooh Bear floated gracefully up into the sky, and stayed there—level with the top of the tree and about twenty feet away from it.

"Hooray!" you shouted.

"Isn't that fine?" shouted Winnie-the-Pooh down to you. "What do I look like?"

"You look like a bear holding on to a balloon," you said.

"Not—" said Pooh anxiously, "—not like a small black cloud in a blue sky?"

"Not very much."

"Ah, well, perhaps from up here it looks different. And, as I say, you never can tell with bees."

There was no wind to blow him nearer to the tree, so there he stayed. He could see the honey, he could smell the honey, but he couldn't quite reach the honey.

After a little while he called down to you.

"Christopher Robin!" he said in a loud whisper.

"Hallo!"

"I think the bees *suspect* something!"

"What sort of thing?"

"I don't know. But something tells me that they're *suspicious*!"

"Perhaps they think that you're after their honey."

"It may be that. You never can tell with bees."

There was another little silence, and then he called down to you again.

"Christopher Robin!"

"Yes?"

"Have you an umbrella in your house?"

"I think so."

"I wish you would bring it out here, and walk up and down with it, and look up at me every now and then, and say 'Tut-tut, it looks like rain.' I think, if you did that, it would help the deception which we are practising on these bees."

Well, you laughed to yourself, "Silly old Bear!" but you didn't say it aloud because you were so fond of him, and you went home for your umbrella.

"Oh, there you are!" called down Winnie-the-Pooh, as soon as you got back to the tree. "I was beginning to get anxious. I have discovered that the bees are now definitely Suspicious."

"Shall I put my umbrella up?" you said.

"Yes, but wait a moment. We must be practical. The important bee to deceive is the Queen Bee. Can you see which is the Queen Bee from down there?"

"No."

"A pity. Well, now, if you walk up and down with your umbrella, saying, 'Tut-tut, it looks like rain,' I shall do what I can by singing a little Cloud Song, such as a cloud might sing. . . . Go!"

So, while you walked up and down and wondered if it would rain, Winnie-the-Pooh sang this song:

> How sweet to be a Cloud
> Floating in the Blue!
> Every little cloud
> *Always* sings aloud.
>
> "How sweet to be a Cloud
> Floating in the Blue!"
> It makes him very proud
> To be a little cloud.

The bees were still buzzing as suspiciously as ever. Some of them, indeed, left their nest and flew all round the cloud as it began the second verse of this song, and one bee sat down on the nose of the cloud for a moment, and then got up again.

"Christopher—*ow!*—Robin," called out the cloud.

"Yes?"

"I have just been thinking, and I have come to a very important decision. *These are the wrong sort of bees.*"

"Are they?"

"Quite the wrong sort. So I should think they would make the wrong sort of honey, shouldn't you?"

"Would they?"

"Yes. So I think I shall come down."

"How?" asked you.

Winnie-the-Pooh hadn't thought about this. If he let go of the string, he would fall—*bump*—and he didn't like the idea of that. So he thought for a long time, and then he said:

"Christopher Robin, you must shoot the balloon with your gun. Have you got your gun?"

"Of course I have," you said. "But if I do that, it will spoil the balloon," you said.

"But if you *don't*," said Pooh, "I shall have to let go, and that would spoil *me.*"

When you put it like this, you saw how it was, and you aimed very carefully at the balloon, and fired.

"Ow!" said Pooh.

"Did I miss?" you asked.

"You didn't exactly miss," said Pooh, "but you missed the *balloon.*"

"I'm so sorry," you said, and you fired again, and this time you hit the balloon, and the air came slowly out, and Winnie-the-Pooh floated down to the ground.

But his arms were so stiff from holding on to the string of the balloon all that time that they stayed up straight in the air for more than a week, and whenever a fly came and settled on his nose he had to blow it off. And I think—but I am not sure—that *that* is why he was always called Pooh.

"Is that the end of the story?" asked Christopher Robin.

"That's the end of that one. There are others."

"About Pooh and Me?"

"And Piglet and Rabbit and all of you. Don't you remember?"

"I do remember, and then when I try to remember, I forget."

"That day when Pooh and Piglet tried to catch the Heffalump——"

"They didn't catch it, did they?"

"No."

"Pooh couldn't, because he hasn't any brain. Did *I* catch it?"

"Well, that comes into the story."

Christopher Robin nodded.

"I do remember," he said, "only Pooh doesn't very well, so that's why he likes having it told to him again. Because then it's a real story and not just a remembering."

"That's just how *I* feel," I said.

Christopher Robin gave a deep sigh, picked his Bear up by the leg, and walked off to the door, trailing Pooh behind him. At the door he turned and said, "Coming to see me have my bath?"

"I might," I said.

"I didn't hurt him when I shot him, did I?"

"Not a bit."

He nodded and went out, and in a moment I heard Winnie-the-Pooh—*bump, bump, bump*—going up the stairs behind him.

BEHIND THE FUR
Winnie-the-Pooh

In August, 1921, Daphne Milne, the wife of author and playwright A. A. Milne, bought a teddy bear for her son's first birthday. It was an English-made Farnell bear from Harrods, a fine department store in London. The teddy bear was exactly the same size as the baby, Christopher Robin.

Perhaps the most famous portrait of A. A. Milne, Christopher Robin Milne, and Winnie-the-Pooh

Christopher Milne and his teddy bear playing in the woods

Christopher treasured his bear. He called him Edward, Teddy, or Big Bear. Many years later, he wrote, "The bear took his place in the nursery and gradually he began to come to life.... As I played with [the toys] and talked to them and gave them voices to answer with, so they began to breathe." As Christopher's father listened to his son's play conversations, he was inspired to write poems and stories based on the bear and the other toys. In his most famous book, Edward was given a new name, Winnie-the-Pooh.

Where did this fancy name come from? It was borrowed from a Canadian bear and an English swan.

The real bear's story begins in Canada in 1914. A young army officer was traveling from Winnipeg to Quebec to join the Second Canadian Infantry Brigade. When Lieutenant Harry D. Colebourn

Winnie, the orphaned cub, and Lieutenant Colebourn on Salisbury Plain, December 1914

changed trains in rural White River, he noticed a hunter with a bear cub tied to the arm of a bench. Lieutenant Colebourn, who had trained as a veterinarian and had a special interest in animals, paid twenty dollars for the orphaned cub and named her Winnie, after Winnipeg. When she arrived in Quebec, she became the mascot of the brigade. Several months later, when the soldiers were shipped to England and then France to fight in World War I, Lieutenant Colebourn left Winnie at the London Zoo for safekeeping.

The bear was extremely popular because she was so gentle. Christopher Milne, one of her many visitors, was allowed to feed Winnie by hand and even to hug her.

Christopher also liked to feed a swan that lived in Kensington Gardens, a London park. He called him Pooh. As his father pointed out, it was a good name for a swan, "because, if you call him and he doesn't come (which is a thing swans are good at), then you can pretend that you were just saying 'Pooh!' to show how little you wanted him."

So the names "Winnie" and "Pooh" were combined and given to Edward Bear. Today he sits in a glass case in the Donnell branch of the New York Public Library. He looks a little worn and bald in places, but visitors agree that he is one of the most adored teddy bears in the world.

Christopher Robin Milne's toys: Tigger, Kanga, Pooh, Piglet, and Eeyore, and the books that describe their adventures

·TEDDY BEAR·

by A. A. Milne
with decorations by Ernest H. Shepard

A bear, however hard he tries,
Grows tubby without exercise.
Our Teddy Bear is short and fat
Which is not to be wondered at;
He gets what exercise he can
By falling off the ottoman,
But generally seems to lack
The energy to clamber back.

Now tubbiness is just the thing
Which gets a fellow wondering;
And Teddy worried lots about
The fact that he was rather stout.
He thought: "If only I were thin!
But how does anyone begin?"
He thought: "It really isn't fair
To grudge me exercise and air."

For many weeks he pressed in vain
His nose against the window-pane,
And envied those who walked about
Reducing their unwanted stout.
None of the people he could see
"Is quite" (he said) "as fat as me!"
Then, with a still more moving sigh,
"I mean" (he said) "as fat as I!"

Now Teddy, as was only right,
Slept in the ottoman at night,
And with him crowded in as well
More animals than I can tell;
Not only these, but books and things,
Such as a kind relation brings—
Old tales of "Once upon a time,"
And history retold in rhyme.

One night it happened that he took
A peep at an old picture-book,
Wherein he came across by chance
The picture of a King of France
(A stoutish man) and, down below,
These words: "King Louis So and So,
Nicknamed 'The Handsome'"! There he sat,
And (think of it!) the man was fat!

Our bear rejoiced like anything
To read about this famous King,
Nicknamed "The Handsome." There he sat,
And certainly the man was fat.
Nicknamed "The Handsome." Not a doubt
The man was definitely stout.
Why then, a bear (for all his tub)
Might yet be named "The Handsome Cub"!

"Might yet be named." Or did he mean
That years ago he "might have been"?
For now he felt a slight misgiving:
"Is Louis So and So still living?
Fashions in beauty have a way
Of altering from day to day.
Is 'Handsome Louis' with us yet?
Unfortunately I forget."

Next morning (nose to window-pane)
The doubt occurred to him again.
One question hammered in his head:
"Is he alive or is he dead?"
Thus, nose to pane, he pondered; but
The lattice window, loosely shut,
Swung open. With one startled "Oh!"
Our Teddy disappeared below.

There happened to be passing by
A plump man with a twinkling eye,
Who, seeing Teddy in the street,
Raised him politely to his feet,
And murmured kindly in his ear
Soft words of comfort and of cheer:
"Well, well!" "Allow me!" "Not at all."
"Tut-tut! A very nasty fall."

Our Teddy answered not a word;
It's doubtful if he even heard.
Our bear could only look and look:
The stout man in the picture-book!
That "handsome" King—could this be he,
This man of adiposity?
"Impossible," he thought. "But still,
No harm in asking. Yes I will!"

"Are you," he said, "by any chance
His Majesty the King of France?"
The other answered, "I am that,"
Bowed stiffly, and removed his hat;
Then said, "Excuse me," with an air,
"But is it Mr. Edward Bear?"
And Teddy, bending very low,
Replied politely, "Even so!"

They stood beneath the window there,

The King and Mr. Edward Bear,

And, handsome, if a trifle fat,

Talked carelessly of this and that....

Then said His Majesty, "Well, well,

I must get on," and rang the bell.

"Your bear, I think," he smiled. "Good-day!"

And turned, and went upon his way.

A bear, however hard he tries,

Grows tubby without exercise.

Our Teddy Bear is short and fat,

Which is not to be wondered at.

But do you think it worries him

To know that he is far from slim?

No, just the other way about—

He's *proud* of being short and stout.

· U S T W O ·

by A. A. Milne
with decorations by Ernest H. Shepard

Wherever I am, there's always Pooh,
There's always Pooh and Me.
Whatever I do, he wants to do,
"Where are you going today?" says Pooh:
"Well, that's very odd 'cos I was too.
Let's go together," says Pooh, says he.
"Let's go together," says Pooh.

"What's twice eleven?" I said to Pooh.
("Twice what?" said Pooh to Me.)
"I *think* it ought to be twenty-two."
"Just what I think myself," said Pooh.
"It wasn't an easy sum to do,
But that's what it is," said Pooh, said he.
"That's what it is," said Pooh.

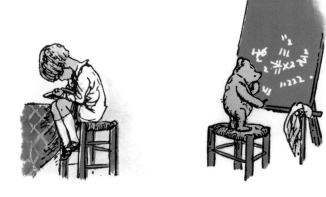

"Let's look for dragons," I said to Pooh.
"Yes, let's," said Pooh to Me.
We crossed the river and found a few—
"Yes, those are dragons all right," said Pooh.
"As soon as I saw their beaks I knew.
That's what they are," said Pooh, said he.
"That's what they are," said Pooh.

"Let's frighten the dragons," I said to Pooh.
"That's right," said Pooh to Me.
"*I'm* not afraid," I said to Pooh,
And I held his paw and I shouted "Shoo!
Silly old dragons!"—and off they flew.
"I wasn't afraid," said Pooh, said he,
"I'm *never* afraid with you."

So wherever I am, there's always Pooh,
There's always Pooh and Me.
"What would I do?" I said to Pooh,
"If it wasn't for you," and Pooh said: "True,
It isn't much fun for One, but Two
Can stick together," says Pooh, says he.
"That's how it is," says Pooh.

Fearless Bears

Titanic Bear

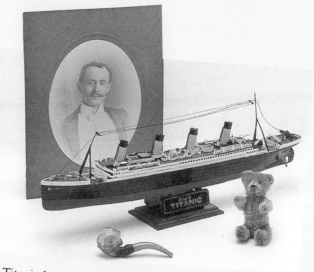

The Titanic *bear with Gaspare Gatti's carved meerschaum pipe, as they appeared in the auction catalog*

Not every teddy bear has happy adventures. One bear was a passenger on the *Titanic,* the ocean liner that sank in the North Atlantic in 1912. The very same bear survived the bombing of London in World War II.

In 1907, a little boy named Vittorio Gatti received a special gift from his uncle, a six-inch gold mohair teddy bear with black metal eyes. Five years later, Vittorio's father, Gaspare Gatti, took a position on the *Titanic,* the largest, fastest, most elegant ship of its time. When the elder Gatti departed, his son gave him his teddy bear for good luck.

Four days into its voyage, the *Titanic* struck an iceberg. Although the ship was thought to be unsinkable, it began to take on water. The passengers and crew members gathered on deck. Gaspare Gatti carried his son's good luck bear nestled inside his waterproof tobacco pouch.

Crew members had to wait for the passengers to board the lifeboats first, but there wasn't enough space in the boats for everyone. In less than three hours, the *Titanic* sank, leaving most of the crew and many passengers to perish in the frigid water.

Gaspare Gatti's body was recovered and buried in Nova Scotia, but his belongings were returned to his widow. Inside his tobacco pouch, Edith Gatti discovered the little bear. She would cherish it for the rest of her life.

During World War II, Edith Gatti lived in London. Night after night, she listened to German warplanes passing overhead and bombs exploding around her. Mrs. Gatti's home was destroyed, but she survived along with the teddy bear.

When Edith Gatti died in 1962, the teddy bear was returned to Vittorio. On his death, Vittorio left the *Titanic* bear to his widow, who later donated it to the Museum of Childhood in Ribchester,

England. In 1995, the museum closed and the collection was auctioned off. The records have disappeared along with the fearless bear, but the sad story survives.

Senior Under Officer Edward Bear

Another teddy bear with a knack for survival is Senior Under Officer Edward Bear. His adventures began when he left a toy shop in Abingdon, England, for the Royal Military Academy Sandhurst, the British army's officer training school.

In July 1950, Edward Bear was "rushed posthaste to the airfield, dressed, harnessed, and briefed overnight." The following morning, he made his first jump out of an airplane. He had his own parachute, although occasionally he would descend without it.

Edward Bear had become the mascot of the school's Parachuting Club, renamed the Edward Bear Club. Members wore green ties decorated with silver parachuting teddy bears.

Officer Cadet Edward Bear was often the first one out of the plane. He was filled with sand so that he would fall to earth quickly rather than float indefinitely. According to his records, Edward Bear displayed a technique "all his own" and "showed no semblance of nervousness." Many of his descents were fault-

less, but his records also noted that "he showed a complete indifference to instruction."

Despite the sand, the bear was known to drift off course and miss the target. Sometimes he landed in a tree, but he never panicked.

During a competition between the Edward Bear Club and a club in France, Edward Bear was kidnapped. The crime affected morale, and the British lost. Edward Bear was also taken prisoner by the Royal Marines and various other organizations. Fortunately, he was always able to escape.

The teddy bear was promoted to Junior Under Officer, then Senior Under Officer. After forty years and four hundred jumps, he retired to the Sandhurst Museum. (His replacement, Officer Cadet Bear, Jr., arrived in 1992.) Although SUO Edward Bear had lost an eye as well as the end of his nose, he had served the academy far longer than any other cadet.

One of the bears is the original SUO Edward Bear. The other is his replacement. Can you tell which is which?

·THE TEDDY· BEARS' PICNIC

lyrics by Jimmy Kennedy, music by J. K. Bratton
illustrated by Bernadette Pons

In 1907, American composer J. K. Bratton wrote a song without words called "The Teddy Bear Two Step." America was at the height of teddy bear mania—women carried teddy bear pocketbooks, and men toted teddy bear briefcases. There were teddy bear tea sets, hammocks, and headlamps for automobiles. And when Teddy Roosevelt stood up to give a speech, guess which song was played?

Twenty-three years later Jimmy Kennedy, an Englishman, wrote words to go with the melody and gave the song a new title, "The Teddy Bears' Picnic." When it was performed on English radio in 1932, it was a smash hit.

If you go down in the woods to-day, you're sure of a big sur-

prise. _____ If you go down in the woods to-day, you'd bet-ter go in dis-

guise. _____ For ev-'ry bear that ev-er there was will gath-er there, for

cer-tain, be-cause to-day's the day the ted-dy bears have their pic - nic.

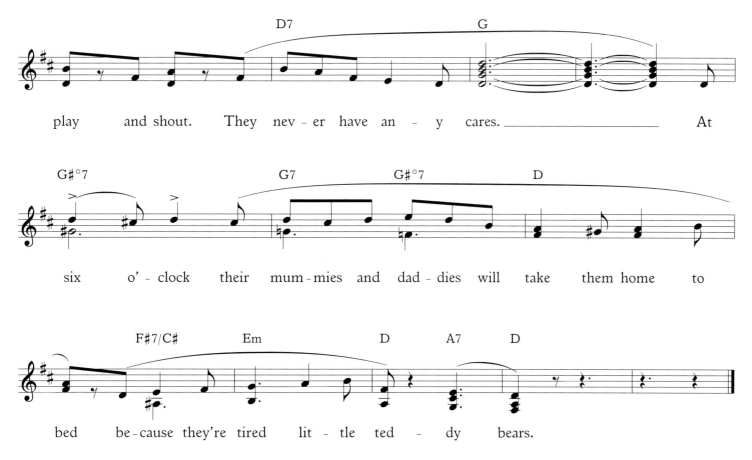

play   and shout.   They   nev - er   have   an - y   cares. _____   At

six   o' - clock   their   mum - mies   and   dad - dies   will   take   them home   to

bed   be - cause   they're   tired   lit - tle   ted - dy   bears.

(Second verse)

Ev'ry teddy bear who's been good

Is sure of a treat today.

There's lots of marvelous things to eat

And wonderful games to play.

Beneath the trees where nobody sees,

They'll hide and seek as long as they please.

'Cause that's the way the teddy bears have their picnic.

Chorus

(Third verse)

If you go down in the woods today,

You'd better not go alone.

It's lovely down in the woods today

But safer to stay at home.

For ev'ry bear that ever there was

Will gather there, for certain, because

Today's the day the teddy bears have their picnic.

Chorus

A BEAR CALLED PADDINGTON

A Shopping Expedition

by Michael Bond
with illustrations by Peggy Fortnum

T he man in the gentlemen's department at Barkridges held Paddington's hat at arm's length between thumb and forefinger. He looked at it distastefully.

"I take it the young…er, gentleman will not be requiring this any more, modom?" he said.

"Oh yes, I shall," said Paddington firmly. "I've always had that hat—ever since I was small."

"But wouldn't you like a nice new one, Paddington?" said Mrs. Brown, adding hastily, "For *best?*"

Paddington thought for a moment. "I'll have one for *worst* if you like," he said. "*That's* my best one!"

The salesman shuddered slightly

and, averting his gaze, placed the offending article on the far end of the counter.

"Albert!" He beckoned to a youth who was hovering in the background. "See what we have in size 4⅞." Albert began to rummage under the counter.

"And now, while we're about it," said Mrs. Brown, "we'd like a nice warm coat for the winter. Something like a duffle coat with toggles so that he can do it up easily, I thought. And we'd also like a plastic raincoat for the summer."

The salesman looked at her haughtily. He wasn't very fond of bears, and this one especially had been giving him funny looks ever since he'd mentioned his wretched hat. "Has modom tried the bargain basement?" he began. "Something in government surplus…"

"No, I haven't," said Mrs. Brown hotly. "Government surplus indeed! I've never heard of such a thing—have you, Paddington?"

"No," said Paddington, who had no idea what government surplus was. *"Never!"* He stared hard at the man, who looked away uneasily. Paddington had a very persistent stare when he cared to use it. It was a very powerful stare. One that his Aunt Lucy had taught him and that he kept for special occasions.

Mrs. Brown pointed to a smart blue duffle coat with a red lining. "That looks the very thing," she said.

The man gulped. "Yes, modom. Certainly, modom." He beckoned to Paddington. "Come this way, sir."

Paddington followed the salesman, keeping about two feet behind him and staring very hard. The back of the man's neck seemed to go a dull red, and he fingered his collar nervously. As they passed the hat counter, Albert, who lived in constant fear of his superior and who had been watching events with an open mouth, gave Paddington the thumbs-up sign. Paddington waved a paw. He was beginning to enjoy himself.

He allowed the salesman to help him on with the coat and then stood admiring himself in the mirror. It was the first coat he had ever possessed. In Peru it had been very hot, and though his Aunt Lucy had made him wear a hat to prevent sunstroke, it had always been much too warm for a coat of any sort. He looked at himself in the mirror and was surprised to see not one but a long line of bears stretching away as far as the eye could see. In fact, everywhere he looked there were bears, and they were all looking extremely smart.

"Isn't the hood a trifle large?" asked Mrs. Brown anxiously.

"Hoods are being worn large this year,

modom," said the salesman. "It's the latest fashion." He was about to add that Paddington seemed to have quite a large head anyway, but he changed his mind. Bears were rather unpredictable. You never quite knew what they were thinking, and this one in particular seemed to have a mind of his own.

"Do *you* like it, Paddington?" asked Mrs. Brown.

Paddington gave up counting bears in the mirror and turned around to look at the back view. "I think it's the nicest coat I've ever seen," he said after a moment's thought. Mrs. Brown and the salesman heaved a sigh of relief.

"Good," said Mrs. Brown. "That's settled, then. Now there's just the question of a hat and a plastic mackintosh."

She walked over to the hat counter, where Albert, who could still hardly take his admiring eyes off Paddington, had arranged a huge pile of hats. There were bowler hats, sun hats, trilby hats, berets, and even a very small top hat. Mrs. Brown eyed them doubtfully. "It's difficult," she said, looking at Paddington. "It's largely a question of his ears. They stick out, rather."

"You could cut some holes for them," said Albert.

The salesman froze him with a glance. "Cut

a hole in a *Barkridges'* hat!" he exclaimed. "I've never heard of such a thing."

Paddington turned and stared at him. "I... er..." The salesman's voice trailed off. "I'll go and fetch my scissors," he said in a strange voice.

"I don't think that will be necessary at all," said Mrs. Brown hurriedly. "It's not as if he had to go to work in the city, so he doesn't want anything too formal. I think this woolen beret is very nice. The one with the pompom on top. The green will go well with his new coat, and it'll stretch so that he can pull it down over his ears when it gets cold."

Everyone agreed that Paddington looked very smart, and while Mrs. Brown looked for a plastic mackintosh, he trotted off to have another look at himself in the mirror. He found the beret was a little difficult to raise, as his ears kept the bottom half firmly in place. But by pulling on the pompom he could make it stretch quite a long way, which was almost as good. It meant, too, that he could be polite without getting his ears cold.

The salesman wanted to wrap up the duffle coat for him, but after a lot of fuss it was agreed that even though it was a warm day, he should wear it. Paddington felt very proud of himself, and he was anxious to see if other people noticed.

After shaking hands with Albert, Paddington gave the salesman one more long, hard stare, and the unfortunate man collapsed into a chair and began mopping his brow as Mrs. Brown led the way out the door.

Barkridges was a large store, and it had its own escalator as well as several elevators. Mrs. Brown hesitated at the door and then took Paddington's paw firmly in her hand and led him toward the elevator. She'd had enough of escalators for one day.

But to Paddington everything was new, or almost everything, and he liked trying strange things. After a few seconds he decided quite definitely that he preferred riding on an escalator. They were nice and smooth. But elevators! To start with, it was full of people carrying parcels and all so busy they had no time to notice a small bear; one woman even rested her shopping bag on his head and seemed quite surprised when Paddington pushed it off. Then suddenly half of him seemed to fall away while the other half stayed where it was. Just as he had got used to that feeling, the second half of him caught up again and even overtook the first half before the doors opened. It did that four times on the way down, and Paddington was glad when they reached the ground floor and Mrs. Brown led him out.

She looked at him closely. "Oh dear, Paddington, you look quite pale," she said. "Are you all right?"

"I feel sick," said Paddington. "I don't like elevators. And I wish I hadn't had such a big breakfast!"

"Oh dear!" Mrs. Brown looked around. Judy, who had gone off to do some shopping of her own, was nowhere to be seen. "Will you be all right sitting here for a few minutes while I find Judy?" she asked.

Paddington sank down onto his case, looking very mournful. Even the pompom on his hat seemed limp.

"I don't know whether I shall be all right," he said. "But I'll do my best."

"I'll be as quick as I can," said Mrs. Brown. "Then we can take a taxi home for lunch."

Paddington groaned.

"Poor Paddington," said Mrs. Brown, "you must be feeling bad if you don't want any lunch."

As he heard the word again, Paddington closed his eyes and gave an even louder groan. Mrs. Brown tiptoed away.

Paddington kept his eyes closed for several minutes, and then, as he began to feel better,

he gradually became aware that every now and then a nice cool draft of air blew over his face. He opened one eye carefully to see where it was coming from and noticed for the first time that he was sitting near the main entrance to the store. He opened his other eye and decided to investigate. If he stayed just

outside the glass door, he could still see Mrs. Brown and Judy when they came.

And then, as he bent down to pick up his suitcase, everything suddenly went black. "Oh dear," thought Paddington, "now all the lights have gone out."

He began groping his way with outstretched paws toward the door. He gave a push where he thought it ought to be, but nothing happened. He tried moving along the wall a little way and gave another push. This time it did move. The door seemed to have a strong spring on it and he had to push hard to make it open, but eventually there was a gap big enough for him to squeeze through. It clanged shut behind him, and Paddington was disappointed to find it was just as dark outside as it had been in the store. He began to wish he'd stayed where he was. He turned around and tried to find the door, but it seemed to have disappeared.

He decided it might be easier if he got down on his paws and crawled. He went a little way like this and then his head came up against something hard. He tried to push it to one side with his paw and it moved slightly, so he pushed again.

Suddenly there was a noise like thunder, and before he knew where he was, a whole mountain of things began to fall on him.

It felt as if the whole sky had fallen in. Everything went quiet and he lay where he was for a few minutes with his eyes tightly shut, hardly daring to breathe. From a long way away he could hear voices, and once or twice it sounded as if someone were banging on a window. He opened one eye carefully and was surprised to find the lights had come on again. At least… Sheepishly, he pushed the hood of his duffle coat up over his head. They hadn't gone out at all! His hood must have fallen over his head when he bent down inside the store to pick up his case.

Paddington sat up and looked around to see where he was. He felt much better now. Somewhat to his astonishment, he found he was sitting in a small room in the middle of which was a great pile of tins and basins and bowls. He rubbed his eyes and stared, round-eyed, at the sight.

Behind him was a wall with a door in it, and in front of him was a large window. On the other side of the window a large crowd of people were pushing one another and pointing in his direction. Paddington decided with pleasure that they must be pointing at him. He stood up with difficulty, because it was hard standing up straight on top of a lot of tins, and pulled the pompom on his hat as high as it would go. A cheer went up from the crowd. Paddington gave a bow, waved several times, and then started to examine the damage all around him.

For a moment he wasn't quite sure where he was, and then it came to him. Instead of going out into the street, he must have opened a door leading to one of the store windows!

Paddington was an observant bear, and since he had arrived in London he'd noticed lots of these windows. They were very interesting. They always had so many things inside them to look at. Once he'd seen a man working in one, piling tin cans and boxes on top of each other to make a pyramid. He remembered deciding at the time what a nice job it must be.

He looked around thoughtfully. "Oh dear," he said to the world in general, "I'm in trouble again." If he'd knocked all these things down, as he supposed he must have done, someone was going to be cross. In fact, lots of people were going to be cross. People weren't very good at having things explained to them, and it was going to be difficult explaining how his duffle coat hood had fallen over his head.

He bent down and began to pick up the things. There were some glass shelves lying on the floor where they had fallen. It was getting warm inside the window, so he took off his duffle coat and hung it carefully on a nail.

Then he picked up a glass shelf and tried balancing it on top of some tins. It seemed to work, so he put some more tins and a bowl on top of that. It was rather wobbly, but… He stood back and examined it. Yes, it looked quite nice. There was an encouraging round of applause from outside. Paddington waved a paw at the crowd and picked up another shelf.

Inside the shop, Mrs. Brown was having an earnest conversation with the store detective.

"You say you left him here, madam?" the detective was saying.

"That's right," said Mrs. Brown. "He was feeling ill and I *told* him not to go away. His name's Paddington."

"Paddington." The detective wrote it carefully in his notebook. "What sort of bear is he?"

"Oh, he's sort of golden," said Mrs. Brown. "He was wearing a blue duffle coat and carrying a suitcase."

"And he has black ears," said Judy. "You can't mistake him."

"Black ears," the detective repeated, licking his pencil.

"I don't expect that'll help much," said Mrs. Brown. "He was wearing his beret."

The detective cupped his hand over his ear. "His *what*?" he shouted. There really was a terrible noise coming from somewhere. It seemed to be getting worse every minute. Every now and then there was a round of applause, and several times he distinctly heard the sound of people cheering.

"His *beret*," shouted Mrs. Brown in return. "A green woolen one that came down over his ears. With a pompom."

The detective shut his notebook with a snap. The noise outside was definitely getting worse. "Pardon me," he said sternly. "There's something strange going on that needs investigating."

Mrs. Brown and Judy exchanged glances. The same thought was running through both their minds. They both said "Paddington!" and rushed after the detective. Mrs. Brown clung to the detective's coat and Judy clung to Mrs. Brown's as they forced their way through the crowd on the pavement. Just as they reached the window a tremendous cheer went up.

"I might have known," said Mrs. Brown.

"Paddington!" exclaimed Judy.

Paddington had just reached the top of his pyramid. At least, it had started off as a pyramid, but it wasn't really. It wasn't any particular shape at all, and it was very rickety. Having placed the last tin on the top, Paddington was in trouble. He wanted to get down, but he couldn't. He reached out a paw and the mountain began to wobble. Paddington clung helplessly to the tins, swaying to and fro, watched by a fascinated audience. And then, without any warning, the whole lot collapsed again, only this time Paddington was on top and not underneath. A groan of disappointment went up from the crowd.

"Best thing I've seen in years," said a man in the crowd to Mrs. Brown. "Blessed if I know how they think these things up."

"Will he do it again, Mummy?" asked a small boy.

"I don't think so, dear," said his mother. "I think he's finished for the day." She pointed to the window, where the detective was removing a sorry-looking Paddington. Mrs. Brown hurried back to the entrance, followed by Judy.

Inside the store the detective looked at Paddington and then at his notebook. "Blue duffle coat," he said. "Green woolen beret!" He pulled the beret off. "Black ears! I know who you are," he said grimly. "You're Paddington!"

Paddington nearly fell over backward with astonishment.

"However did you know that?" he said.

"I'm a detective," said the man. "It's my job to know these things. We're always on the lookout for criminals."

"But I'm not a criminal," said Paddington hotly. "I'm a bear! Besides, I was only tidying up the window…"

"Tidying up the window," the detective sputtered. "I don't know what Mr. Perkins will have to say. He only dressed it this morning."

Paddington looked around uneasily. He could see Mrs. Brown and Judy hurrying toward him. In fact, there were several people coming his way, including an important-looking man in a black coat and striped trousers. They all reached him at the same time and all began talking together.

Paddington sat down on his case and watched them. There were times when it was much better to keep quiet, and this was one of them. In the end it was the important-looking man who won, because he had the loudest voice and kept on talking when everyone else had finished.

To Paddington's surprise, he reached down, took hold of his paw, and started to shake it so hard he thought it was going to drop off.

"Delighted to know you, bear," he boomed. "Delighted to know you. And congratulations."

"That's all right," said Paddington doubtfully. He didn't know why, but the man seemed very pleased.

The man turned to Mrs. Brown. "You say his name's Paddington?"

"That's right," said Mrs. Brown. "And I'm sure he didn't mean any harm."

"Harm?" The man looked at Mrs. Brown in amazement. "Did you say *harm?* My dear lady, through the action of this bear we've had the biggest crowd in years. Our telephone hasn't stopped ringing." He waved toward the entrance to the store. "And still they come!"

He placed his hand on Paddington's head. "Barkridges," he said, "Barkridges is grateful!" He waved his other hand for silence. "We should like to show our gratitude. If there is anything—anything in the store you would like…?"

Paddington's eyes gleamed. He knew just what he wanted. He'd seen it on their way up to the men's department. It had been standing all by itself on a counter in the food store. The biggest one he'd ever seen. Almost as big as himself.

"Please," he said, "I'd like one of those jars of marmalade. One of the big ones."

If the manager of Barkridges felt surprised, he didn't show it. He stood respectfully to one side, by the entrance to the elevator.

"Marmalade it shall be," he said, pressing the button.

"I think," said Paddington, "if you don't mind, I'd rather use the stairs."

BEHIND THE FUR
Paddington

On Christmas Eve, 1956, writer Michael Bond missed a bus in London. He slipped into Selfridges, a department store, to get out of the sleet and to buy his wife a last-minute gift. In the toy department, he discovered a teddy bear sitting alone on a shelf. Mr. Bond bought the bear for his wife, and together they named him Paddington after a nearby railroad station.

The following spring, Mr. Bond was staring at a blank piece of paper, wondering what to write next, when he noticed the teddy bear. He typed: "Mr. and Mrs. Brown first met Paddington on a railway platform"—the opening words of his much-loved book, *A Bear Called Paddington*. In an early draft, Paddington came from Darkest Africa. When Mr. Bond learned that there are no bears in Africa, Paddington's birthplace moved to Darkest Peru. Although the stories of Paddington were inspired by a teddy bear, and although stuffed bears with his distinctive duffle coat, wide-brimmed hat, and Wellington boots can be found in many toy stores, Mr. Bond insists that Paddington is not a teddy bear. He is a real bear!

Michael Bond and a large Paddington

The Teddy Bear Invasion

illustrated by Elisabeth Schlossberg

In September, 1993, a tugboat pulled a barge away from a dock in New Jersey. The barge carried metal containers, packed with cardboard boxes. Inside, thousands of teddy bears lay side by side—small bears as white as marshmallows and larger ones the color of cinnamon. Each bear wore a blue and red sweater with a diamond pattern on the front.

The bears were on their way to department stores in New England in time for the Christmas shopping season. As they passed the tip of Long Island, black clouds appeared on the horizon.

There was a flash of lightning, a crack, and a low rumble. Waves jostled the tug and washed over the deck of the barge. The chains holding the metal containers squealed like pigs.

A twelve-foot wave smashed into the barge and rolled over the deck. Chains snapped, and thirty-one containers slid into the ocean. As the containers sank, their lids came off. The cardboard boxes inside rose to the surface and bobbed like apples.

Soon the cardboard softened and sank, leaving thousands of teddy bears behind. They rode the waves, up the front and down the back. They twirled, crisscrossed, and bumped heads. Some stared at the grizzly sky, others at the seaweed far below. As the storm moved out to sea, the slick of bears made its way toward the shores of a small town in Rhode Island.

Waves crashed onto the beach and slid backward. Each one left dozens of bears on the sand. People arrived from near and far to see the furry castaways. They brought large garbage bags, filled them with soggy bears, and carried them home.

The bears swirled in washing machines, thumped in dryers, and hung by their ears from clotheslines. When they were dry, they were wrapped in Christmas paper and hidden in closets, or mailed to friends and grandparents far away. Many of the bears were donated to homeless shelters and day-care centers.

Everyone in town kept at least one teddy bear. Today, they sit on mantelpieces and television sets, next to the cash register at the local garage, and near the teller at the bank. Occasionally, a stranger will ask, "Why do you have a teddy bear?"

The answer is always the same: "The Teddy Bear Invasion! Haven't you heard of the Teddy Bear Invasion?"

A HUG OF
TEDDY BEAR POEMS

illustrated by Thea Kliros

When teddy bears get together, they're often referred to as a hug of bears.
So, with a little poetic license, here is a hug of teddy bear poems.

Fuzzy Wuzzy

Fuzzy Wuzzy was a bear,
    A bear was Fuzzy Wuzzy.
When Fuzzy Wuzzy lost his hair,
    He wasn't fuzzy, was he?

—Traditional

Hat

Teddy said it was a hat,
So I put it on.
Now Dad is saying,
"Where the heck's
    the toilet plunger gone?"

—Shel Silverstein

Teddy Hall

Teddy Hall
Is so small,
A rat could eat him,
Hat and all.

—Anonymous

—— 44 ——

Teddy Bear Poem

I threw away my teddy bear,
The one that lost his eye.
I threw him in the garbage pail
(I thought I heard him cry.)

I've had that little teddy bear
Since I was only two.
But I'm much bigger now and
I've got better things to do

Than play with silly teddy bears.
And so I said good-bye
And threw him in the garbage pail.
(Who's crying—he, or I?)

—*Judith Viorst*

Teddy Bear, Teddy Bear

Teddy bear, teddy bear,
   turn around.
Teddy bear, teddy bear,
   touch the ground.
Teddy bear, teddy bear,
   go upstairs.
Teddy bear, teddy bear,
   say your prayers.
Teddy bear, teddy bear,
   switch off the light.
Teddy bear, teddy bear,
   say good night.

—*Traditional*

Helping Bears &
Bears Helping

Teddy bears never grow up, but they do age. A seam lets go and the insides fall out. Bears lose eyes, ears, a leg, and even a face. (Puppies and kittens love teddy bear snouts!) In the past, a chewed bear might be thrown away. Today, he goes to the hospital.

At the Vermont Teddy Bear Company, Nurse Stacey admits injured bears to the BCU, or Bear Care Unit. In four to six weeks, they are shipped back to their owners in a new box with a white hospital bracelet and discharge papers.

Teddy bear hospitals treat bears who have been burned in a fire, attacked by a jealous pet, or spent too many years in an attic. Sometimes, the patient arrives with other stuffed animals to keep him company.

A teddy bear hospital in Ontario, Canada, makes many specialized diagnoses: a bear with a torn seam has "seamitis," and a limp bear needing stuffing gets a "limpectomy." Of course, the bears are always cured.

For those who are afraid to mail their bears to a hospital, there are "walk-in" clinics at teddy bear events.

"What kind of eyes did he have? Shoe button or glass?" a volunteer doctor asks a little girl at a

Susanna, Judi, and a brave bear at a teddy bear clinic

teddy bear rally in Massachusetts. "And was his snout long or short?"

"My bear needs a new mouth," says a boy nearby.

"What kind of mouth?"

The boy's lips form a straight line. "He smiles like this."

Some teddy bear hospitals are not for teddy bears at all. They're real hospitals that use teddy bears to help children. In Norway, Germany, and Israel, boys and girls learn that they don't have to be afraid of doctors, stethoscopes, or eye patches. A doctor will show a young patient how to use a stethoscope on her bear's fuzzy chest. Another puts a black patch on a teddy's plastic eye before giving a boy his own eye patch. It's easier to try something when a teddy bear has done it first.

Teddy bears have often helped people through difficult experiences. When the ship *Titanic* sank in 1912, many of the passengers and crew perished. The Steiff Company created black bears as a tribute to the victims of the disaster. For those who had lost loved ones, the "mourning" bear was something to hold and love.

Karen Braithwaite listening to a mass in honor of firefighters and police officers who perished in the aftermath of the attack on the World Trade Center in New York City

A black "mourning" bear, one of six hundred made by Steiff following the Titanic disaster

After the World Trade Center was destroyed on September 11, 2001, teddy bears were everywhere. In New York City, teddy bears sat on street corners next to photographs, messages, and candles. The Flagg family of Bertram, Texas, brought three thousand teddy bears in ten suitcases to children in New York. More bears arrived from North Dakota and Arizona. Teddy bears with USA on their chests comforted children and adults alike. They represented a belief in America and a connection to a simpler, happier world.

· C O R D U R O Y ·

story and pictures by Don Freeman

C orduroy is a bear who once lived in the toy department of a big store. Day after day he waited with all the other animals and dolls for somebody to come along and take him home.

The store was always filled with shoppers buying all sorts of things, but no one ever seemed to want a small bear in green overalls.

Then one morning a little girl stopped and looked straight into Corduroy's bright eyes.

"Oh, Mommy!" she said. "Look! There's the very bear I've always wanted."

"Not today, dear." Her mother sighed. "I've spent too much already. Besides, he doesn't look new. He's lost the button to one of his shoulder straps."

Corduroy watched them sadly as they walked away.

"I didn't know I'd lost a button," he said to himself. "Tonight I'll go and see if I can find it."

Late that evening, when all the shoppers had gone and the doors were shut and locked, Corduroy carefully climbed down from his shelf and began searching everywhere on the floor for his lost button.

Suddenly he felt the floor moving under him! Quite by accident he had stepped onto an escalator—and up he went!

"Could this be a mountain?" he wondered. "I think I've always wanted to climb a mountain."

He stepped off the escalator as it reached the next floor, and there, before his eyes, was a most amazing sight—tables and chairs and lamps and sofas, and rows and rows of beds.

"This must be a palace!" Corduroy gasped. "I guess I've always wanted to live in a palace."

He wandered around admiring the furniture.

"This must be a bed," he said. "I've always wanted to sleep in a bed." And up he crawled onto a large, thick mattress.

All at once he saw something small and round.

"Why, here's my button!" he cried. And he tried to pick it up. But, like all the other buttons on the mattress, it was tied down tight.

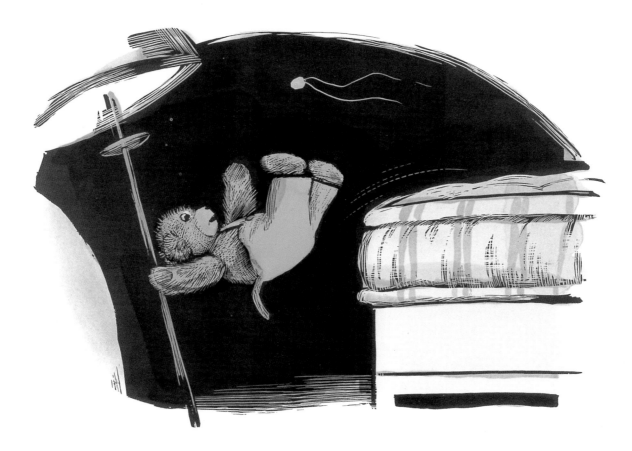

He yanked and pulled with both paws until POP! Off came the button—and off the mattress Corduroy toppled, *bang* into a tall floor lamp. Over it fell with a crash!

Corduroy didn't know it, but there was someone else awake in the store. The night watchman was going his rounds on the floor above. When he heard the crash he came dashing down the escalator.

"Now who in the world did that!" he exclaimed. "Somebody must be hiding around here!"

He flashed his light under and over sofas and beds until he came to the biggest bed of all. And there he saw two fuzzy brown ears sticking up from under the cover.

"Hello!" he said. "How did *you* get upstairs?"

The watchman tucked Corduroy under his arm and carried him down the escalator and set him on the shelf in the toy department with the other animals and dolls.

Corduroy was just waking up when the first customers came into the store in the morning. And there, looking at him with a wide, warm smile, was the same little girl he'd seen only the day before.

"I'm Lisa," she said, "and you're going to be my very own bear. Last night I counted what I've saved in my piggy bank and my mother said I could bring you home."

"Shall I put him in a box for you?" the saleslady asked.

"Oh, no thank you," Lisa answered. And she carried Corduroy home in her arms.

She ran all the way up four flights of stairs, into her family's apartment, and straight to her own room.

Corduroy blinked. There was a chair and a chest of drawers, and alongside a girl-size bed stood a little bed just the right size for him. The room was small, nothing like that enormous palace in the department store.

"This must be home," he said. "I *know* I've always wanted a home!"

Lisa sat down with Corduroy on her lap and began to sew a button on his overalls.

"I like you the way you are," she said, "but you'll be more comfortable with your shoulder strap fastened."

"You must be a friend," said Corduroy. "I've always wanted a friend."

"Me too!" said Lisa, and gave him a big hug.

BEHIND THE FUR
Corduroy

The author, illustrator, and trumpeter Don Freeman

Don Freeman might never have written and illustrated *Corduroy* if he hadn't lost his trumpet. He received the shiny brass horn as a present for his tenth birthday and taught himself to play by listening to records. "After several months, I played along with the best recorded orchestras in the nation," he recalled.

As a young man, Mr. Freeman supported himself with the trumpet. He joined a five-piece band and played in a boxing arena in San Diego. When a fighter went down, the band burst into songs such as "If You Knew Susie."

But Mr. Freeman also loved to draw. He sketched people on the streets and in the theater and sold a few of his images to newspapers in New York. One day Mr. Freeman was busy drawing on the subway when the train reached his stop. He jumped off and left his trumpet behind. He pounded on the door, but the train moved on. He said later, "Losing my horn made me face the fact that I would have to make my living by drawing."

Corduroy was one of the many books Don Freeman wrote and drew for children. When he died in 1978, there were over a million copies of his books in print.

A
Teddy Bear Rally

Welcome to Amherst, Massachusetts! It's a hot Saturday in August, and the town common is blanketed with small white tents. A perky voice is singing "The Teddy Bears' Picnic" over a loudspeaker. You walk to the beat, then suddenly you are surrounded by teddy bears in all colors, shapes, and sizes. It's a teddy bear rally.

In the 1970s, talented artists began to create and sell teddy bears to a growing market of collectors. At a teddy bear rally, artists and collectors come together. They mingle with children searching for a new friend, as well as people of all ages, shapes, and sizes who love and admire teddy bears.

In the first tent, the bears slouch on wooden shelves beneath large photographs of expressionless sheep. The artist, Dianne Stott, straightens a purple bear and explains that she raises the sheep for their fleece, which she spins into yarn, colors with plant dyes, and weaves into teddy bears.

She introduces another

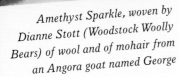

Amethyst Sparkle, woven by Dianne Stott (Woodstock Woolly Bears) of wool and of mohair from an Angora goat named George

bear. "This is Chartreuse Tooloose," she says. "His color came from a wildflower called Queen Anne's lace." Like all her woolly bears, he has a big heart.

A man sells honey in the next tent. You don't have to ask why anyone would sell honey at a teddy bear rally, but, you wonder, where is the marmalade for Paddington?

You pass by bears with goggles and bears in football uniforms. A small table holds teddy bear hats with feathers and diamond pins. Another table exhibits teddy bear shoes, teddy bear salt and pepper shakers, and soap with red and green bears floating inside. You read the words on an overstuffed pillow: MY FAVORITE TREASURES I GLADLY SHARE, EXCEPT OF COURSE MY TEDDY BEAR.

Chartreuse Tooloose, woven by Dianne Stott, from the wool of a sheep named Eloise

In the next tent, you are introduced to two bears, Pete and Repeat. You ask the artist when she decides if her bear is a boy or a girl.

Pete and Repeat, created by a sixteen-year-old artist, Nalene Denning. (Pete has the darker ribbon.)

the color of butterscotch pudding marches at the front, waving vigorously. A five-piece band follows behind, surrounded by barking dogs. Children push baby carriages filled with teddy bears or cradle a bear in their arms.

For some reason, you can't forget the purple bear. Where was she? As you walk from tent to tent, you think, she wasn't the biggest, the best, the softest, or the prettiest. You find the right tent, but the bear is gone.

"Did you sell the purple bear?" you ask.

"Don't worry," the artist replies. "I made sure she was going to a good home."

Trapeze Girl, created by Dianne Liddic (Crafty Frog) for a teddy bear show with a circus theme

"When I'm finished," she answers. "Sometimes, I try very hard to make a girl, but when I'm finished, I put a pink bow around his neck, and he looks funny. The bears tell you who they are."

One tent has old Steiff bears looking tattered and loved. They have no fancy sweaters, no shoes or hats, but they are very valuable.

"How do people decide?" you ask a collector. "There are so many teddy bears."

"The bear has to speak to you," the man replies. "You simply can't leave him behind. There is something in the bear's expression that says, 'You and I should be together.' It's really all about comfort and joy."

The teddy bear parade begins. A huge bear

A teddy bear enthusiast and friend, proudly wearing their handsome hats

Bears Blast into the Future

Astronaut Bear

At the Kennedy Space Center, a calm voice counted, "10...9...8...7..." A short distance away, three engines ignited and roared like beasts. "5...4...3..." Flames and smoke engulfed the launchpad. "2...1..." At 2:19 P.M. on October 29, 1998, Space Shuttle *Discovery* lifted off with the first official teddy bear astronaut on board.

Dr. Mukai and Kumataro floating happily in space

The teddy bear accompanied seven other astronauts into orbit around the earth. He was the "astronaut assistant" of Dr. Chiaki Mukai, a heart surgeon and the first Japanese woman in space. Together they would study the effects of zero gravity on the astronauts.

Zero gravity affects the human body in many different ways. Not only do astronauts float, but their body fluids shift upward. They develop puffy faces and the skinny "chicken legs of space." Of course, Dr. Mukai's assistant had no fluids, so his appearance in space was the same as it was far below.

The teddy bear floated upside down and right side up. As he passed over Europe and the United States, he twirled, flipped, and dove. While the other astronauts were eating dried beef 350 miles above Australia, the teddy bear somersaulted backward.

On the seventh day of the mission, Dr. Mukai decided to name her teddy bear. She asked for suggestions via satellite and received over twenty thousand responses. The winner was "Kumataro." The Japanese word for "bear" is *kuma,* and *taro* is a common ending for a male name.

On the trip, the space shuttle accelerated to 25,000 miles per hour, circled the earth approximately every ninety minutes, and traveled a total of 3.6 million miles. Without a doubt, Kumataro flew faster and farther than any other teddy bear.

Robot Bear

Soon after Kumataro landed at the Kennedy Space Center, another bear began to attract attention in Japan. His name is Kuma, and he can talk, wink, smile, wiggle, and sing.

Kuma is a robot. He was developed by the Matsushita Electric Industrial Company to be a companion to the elderly. By 2005, 20 percent of Japan's population will be sixty-five years old or older. As retirement homes are rare in Japan, many of the elderly will live alone. Who will keep them company? Perhaps it will be a clever blue bear. Just imagine the conversations:

"Ohayo," the old woman says. (That's "good morning" in Japanese.)

"Ohayo," Kuma replies. A microphone in his ears recognizes the woman's words and responds.

The woman pats the bear between the ears. A sensor in his head feels the pat and tells the head, ears, arms, and legs to respond. The bear stirs like a sleeping dog. The woman tickles him behind the ears. Kuma wiggles with joy. A screen on the bear's face lights up with smiling eyes.

Kuma, with his computer inside, is capable of fifty phrases and many simple conversations. The elderly woman loves baseball and wonders how the Japanese pitcher Hideo Nomo is doing. The bear tells her that Nomo had another no-hitter. She asks what the weather will be. Should she go out? Kuma informs her that it will rain all day long, but tomorrow will be better.

At the end of the day, the bear says, *"Oyasumi."* ("Good night.") The panel on his face shows closed eyes. Before he drifts off he sings a children's song, *"Umi ha hiroina, ookiina. Tsuki ga noborushi hi ga shizumu."* ("The sea is big and wide. The moon rises and the sun sets.")

Kuma, the robotic bear. If only you could hear him sing...

Conclusion

Happy one hundredth birthday, teddy bears! It's easy to imagine you clustered around a table, all wearing pointed paper hats, except Paddington, who insists on wearing his own. There's ice cream and cake, of course, with clouds of pink frosting and a teddy bear on top. A jar of honey sits in front of Pooh. He pushes another jar, with marmalade, toward Paddington. The first one to speak is the teddy bear sewn by Rose Michtom.

"Before us," he begins, "they just had dolls. I mean, girls had dolls. Boys had trains and horses on wheels."

"Hard to hug a train," says a Steiff bear. Ice cream drips down his furry chest.

"We were the first toy for both boys and girls," says Fuzzy Wuzzy proudly. He notices that the robotic bear is winking at him. There's something wrong with his computer, Fuzzy Wuzzy decides.

"Some of us were never a toy for children," says SUO Edward Bear as he adjusts the patch over his eye. "We were for grown-ups."

"And old people," adds the robotic bear. "Everyone loves teddy bears. Not everyone loves dolls." A wink turns to smiling eyes on his display panel.

"There's lots to celebrate," says the *Titanic* bear. "We've been around for good times…" He glances at Kumataro.

Kumataro grins. "I did one hundred and eighty-seven somersaults in space," he brags.

"And bad times," *Titanic* bear says sadly.

Pooh, the Bear of Very Little Brain, who can be very wise, says, "And they never forget us."

It is quiet for a moment except for the clinking of spoons on dessert plates. Paddington climbs onto the table to reach his marmalade. A paw slips into the bowl of ice cream, but no one seems to notice.

"What do you think teddy bears will be like a hundred years from now?" asks a bear who is still full from the teddy bears' picnic.

The Michtoms' bear thinks for a moment and then replies, "We'll be just the same, but everything else will be different." The other bears nod in agreement and reach for more cake.

Bibliography

"A Bear with a Future." *The Wish Stream* (March, 1951).

Bjork, Christina. *Big Bear's Book by Himself*. Stockholm, Sweden: R. & S. Books, 1994.

Brown, Michele. *The Teddy Bear Hall of Fame: A Century of Historic Bears*. London: Headline Book Publishing, 1996.

Bull, Peter. *The Teddy Bear Book*. New York: Random House, 1970.

Cockrill, Pauline. *The Ultimate Teddy Bear Book*. New York: Dorling Kindersley, 1991.

Denison, Lindsay. "President Roosevelt's Mississippi Bear Hunt." *Outing* (February 1903).

Dickinson, Judge Jacob M. "Stories and Reminiscences: Theodore Roosevelt's Mississippi Bear Hunt." *Outdoor America* (April 1924).

Greene, Carol. *Margarete Steiff: Toy Maker*. Chicago: Children's Press, 1993.

Melrose, A. R. *The Pooh Bedside Reader*. New York: Dutton, 1996.

Milne, A. A. *When We Were Very Young*. New York: E. P. Dutton & Co., 1924.

Milne, Christopher. *The Enchanted Places*. London: Methuen, 1974.

Mullins, Linda. *The Teddy Bear Men: Theodore Roosevelt & Clifford Berryman*. Hobby House Press, 1987.

Stanford, Maureen, and Amanda O'Neill. *The Teddy Bear Book*. North Dighton, MA: J.G. Press, 1995.

Taylor, Catherine. *Teddy Bear Stories for Grown-Ups*. Golden, CO: Fulcrum Publishing, 1994.

Thwaite, Ann. *The Brilliant Career of Winnie-the-Pooh*. New York: Dutton, 1992.

Waring, Philippa, and Peter Waring. *Teddy Bears*. London: Treasury Press, 1984.